10 09 08   8 7 6 5

Published by
Gibbs Smith, Publisher
P.O. Box 667
Layton, Utah 84041

www.gibbs-smith.com
Orders: 1.800.748.5439

Printed and bound in China.

Library of Congress Cataloging-in-Publication Data

Phillips, Betty Lou.
Emily goes wild! / Betty Lou Phillips ; illustrations by Sharon Watts.—1st ed.
p. cm.
Summary: A pampered monkey living with a dressmaker in New Orleans, Louisiana, begins to
act like a wild animal and must be taken to the zoo.

ISBN 10: 1-58685-268-X   ISBN 13: 978-1-58685-268-9
1. Monkeys—Juvenile fiction. [1. Monkeys—Fiction. 2. Wild animals as pets—Fiction.
3. Pets—Fiction. 4. Zoos—Fiction. 5. New Orleans (La.)—Fiction.]
I. Watts, Sharon, ill.
II. Title.
PZ10.3.P344Em 2003
[Fic]—dc21
2003004844

Emily goes Wild

an Exotic Tail

with a french Twist

Written by **Betty Lou Phillips**

Illustrated by **Sharon Watts**

GIBBS P SMITH

Gibbs Smith, Publisher
Salt Lake City

Emily *twirled* in the mirror. She loved the new tutu Madame DuBois made for her to wear.

Emily had come
to live with Madame
DuBois as a baby, shortly
before the two moved
to New Orleans from Paris.

Madame DuBois loved the little monkey
with all her heart. Often, she worked into the
night stitching pajamas and frilly dresses for
Emily. "Oooo la la. Emily will look divine," she
said. Then she made a polka-dot bikini for her to
brave the summer heat and a shiny red coat with
a hood for rainy days.

Often she looked for new places to hide. Her favorite spots were between the books on a shelf, in a pillowcase, and in the kitchen wastebasket—after she dumped out the trash.

By morning
Emily would again
be her busy self—

putting on makeup,

climbing curtains,

or shredding the daily paper.

Of course, Madame DuBois
could find Emily anywhere.
All she had to do was look
for a dreadful mess.

When Emily was too exhausted to have dinner at

the table, Madame DuBois would say,

"Enjoy your meal,

my darling,"

as she served her in bed.

Au Clair de la Lune...

Like many friends, the two did most everything together. Side by side, they

played the piano,

laced necklaces,

to decorate the house.

CANDY

and painted pictures

They also went to Café Du Monde, in the French Market, for *beignets*—the famous sugar doughnuts.

Sometimes Emily did not feel like walking. So she pretended that she could not take another step. "*Ma chérie*, please get up and come along," Madame DuBois would say. When Emily didn't budge, Madame DuBois would carry her home.

The monkey looked startled. Suddenly, she raced forward. Without warning, Emily grabbed Madame DuBois's favorite bracelet.

Then Emily tore off her glasses and ran into the bathroom with them.

As Madame DuBois stood speechless,

Emily flushed them down the toilet.

"Good grief! What in the world is wrong

with Emily?" she asked.

Mon Dieu!

Minutes later, Madame DuBois was on the telephone with the veterinarian. While they were discussing Emily's behavior, Emily tore the sunflower off Madame DuBois's handbag. "Oh, Dr. Olivier, I must hang up. Thank you for your help," she said.

ma Chérie!

sighed Madame DuBois. "What's the matter, ma petite? Are you no longer happy here? We must find a place for you to be with other monkeys."

After gathering Emily's toys, crayons, and favorite books, she buckled her into a car seat and drove to the city

Zoo →

Hand in hand, the two wound their way through a forest to the zoo office.

"You must promise
to take good care of Emily,"

insisted Madame DuBois,

after telling her story.

"We'll do all we can to give Emily a good home," said

the curator. Then, as tears ran down her cheeks,

Madame DuBois signed the papers donating her monkey

to the zoo. Much as she loved her, clearly Emily was no

longer happy in a house.

As she drove away, Madame DuBois took a last look at the zoo.

"Don't feel sad," she tried telling herself. "Giving up Emily was the right thing to do." Nevertheless, a tear ran down her cheek.

Zoo Exit
Au Revoir!!!

(sniffle)

As a matter of fact, Madame DuBois felt so awful she could not eat. Nor could she sleep. Looking at photos of Emily made her sniffle.

Once Emily drew a
picture with mustard
on the kitchen wall.

Furthermore, Madame DuBois knew that monkeys love to be outdoors where they can climb tall trees, swing from branches, and hide among the bushes. Since Emily lived indoors, it was her nature to climb floor lamps, swing from chandeliers, and hide among the leaves of tall plants.

One H-O-T summer day Madame DuBois called, "Emily, ma chérie, come along to the dress shop."

But Emily was busy. So Madame DuBois called again, this time more firmly.

Emily!

The monkey scurried past Meurice, the house cat, then turned around and pulled his tail.

Emily!!!

screamed Madame DuBois, her patience exhausted.

"Good grief!" Madame DuBois sighed, as she rolled her eyes. "What am I going to do with you, Emily? Every day I spend hours cleaning up."

Madame DuBois rarely scolded her. How could she? She was Emily's only friend. Besides, more than anything, she wanted Emily to be happy.

Soon she forgot everything unpleasant about raising a monkey. Picking up the toys Emily had played with that very morning was more than she could bear. Eventually, she fell asleep on the sofa.

When she awakened, she missed Emily terribly. Did Emily miss her, too? she wondered. What if Emily forgot to pack her blanket? Did she like her new home? She would simply go and see.

ZOO
ENTRANCE

emily

MONKEY JUNGLE ▶

Madame DuBois raced to the zoo.

Once inside, she headed straight for Monkey Jungle.

But before she reached it, she spotted Emily sitting in a cage all by herself, facing a wall.

Out of the corner of her eye, of course, Emily saw Madame DuBois. But the little monkey

would not turn around, no matter how many times Madame DuBois called her name.

Madame DuBois knew why Emily was cross. That morning Emily was given some shots, like all new arrivals. What's more, she would have to live by herself until her caretakers were sure she was healthy. Then she could join the other monkeys.

DAYS

MONKEY JUNGLE

Naturally,
this would be hard
for a little monkey
who was used to enjoying
banana splits, playing dress up,
and annoying the cat.

Emily was not in the habit of being treated like a monkey.

Madame DuBois felt very sad.

Day after day, Madame DuBois went to the zoo hoping a new day would be different. But Emily just ignored her. Madame DuBois was thinking she had made a terrible mistake.

I MUST have my Monkey back!

said Madame DuBois

when she found the groundskeeper.

"Wild animals do not make good house pets," he replied.

"That is one reason we have so many monkeys here.

She will be happy.

Just be patient. You will see."

Madame DuBois was used to getting her way.

"I must do something," she told herself.

MONKEY JUNGLE

But what? Finally, she had a thought. The next day, she headed back to the zoo, past the groundskeeper, straight to the monkey keeper.

"I MUST have my monkey back!" she cried. "I will pay for the food she has eaten. I will buy a tree for the living room. Not only do I miss her, but I feel awful because she is so sad."

"*No* house is big enough for a monkey, even one with a tree," said the monkey keeper, firmly. "Please be patient. You will see. Emily will be happy here. Meanwhile, you may visit Emily as often as you like."

Madame DuBois *still* wasn't sure that leaving Emily at the zoo was the right thing to do.

MONKEYS

The next morning she again drove to the zoo. Past the groundskeeper and monkey keeper she went. Finally, she reached the curator, who was in charge of getting animals for the zoo. Certainly he would understand how she felt. *"Please,* may I have my monkey back?" she begged. "I have tried to be patient, but I am so worried about her that I can hardly sleep."

MONKEY JUNGLE

ZOO TRAIN

he curator
ought for a
oment. Madame
uBois held her
eath.

Then he said, "No doubt about it, the zoo
could operate with one less monkey.
We have plenty of monkeys.

ut I want to show
ou something."
ith that, he led
e way toward
onkey Jungle.

"Oh Emily,
ma chérie, you
look so happy!"
cried Madame DuBois.
"This really is the best
home for you."

Divine!

Voila

From a distance Madame DuBois
could hear Emily chattering. When she
got closer, she saw that Emily was playing
hide-and-seek with the other monkeys.
Suddenly Emily spotted Madame
DuBois, and grabbed a new friend's
hand. Together the monkeys raced
toward her, getting as close as they
could get.

As Emily ate sweet fruits, climbed the sturdy ropes, and swung from the trees, Madame DuBois thought,

"Emily is having more fun here than swinging from a chandelier."

Then, as she watched the little monkey, she had an idea. "How would the zoo like to have a new volunteer?" Madame DuBois asked the curator when he stopped by later that day.

"I could help visitors understand that the zoo is the best place for animals that no longer live in the jungle. At the same time, I would be close to Emily."

The curator's face brightened.

"What a great idea!"

he replied with a smile.

"In fact, you could begin helping right now," he said. "The people across the path just brought in their pet alligator. I think they would enjoy talking with you."